The Christmas BIRD DIARY

Matt Poll

-For my parents-

CHAPTER 1

Montréal, December 14, 1960

Mairin flopped into the lounger and tucked herself deeper into her father's thick terrycloth robe with a shiver. Straining with her bare toes, she pulled the timeworn chair closer to the fireplace, and thought of her father. Randall Lang had survived through two years of war in Europe, but the horrors he had witnessed there caught up to him a decade later, and finally claimed his life.

The living room was flame-flickered a vibrant orange, which caused the Christmas tree's shadow to waver. Mairin put down the binoculars she had been cleaning and chewed on a lock of hair she had twisted around her index finger.

It's like I'm inside one of those hokey glass restaurant candles, Mairin thought.

She took in the smallish spruce tree in the corner, limbs bowing under the weight of the excessive bulbs and tinsel her mother always loaded onto the family Christmas tree. Chunky flakes of snow wafted past the midnight blue Montréal sky through the front picture window, which had frost growing on the inside of the pane.

Maybe it's a snow globe I'm inside of. Guess there are no birds out there for me to count tonight, Mairin mused. She swirled the hot chocolate around in her mug and scrutinized it, then leaned back in her chair. After a moment of perfect balance, the chair tilted too far back, and Mairin's toes lifted off the wood floor. She tried to regain her balance, but the heavy chair's momentum took over. The padded backrest knocked into the bookshelf, causing the central shelf to pop loose with an ominous snap. Almost every book on the shelf slid

1

and toppled to the floor with a dramatic clatter.

Mairin chuckled at the ceiling, then dropped to her knees and began to re-shelve the dozen books on the floor. She picked up one volume and slid it back onto the shelf, but her fingers froze on the rough spine. The scruffy surface revealed an older quality that the other books lacked. Mairin pulled the book back off the shelf and opened it.

"*Christmas Carols, New and Old*, from ... 1871, wow," Mairin cooed under her breath as her eyes narrowed, fixating on the sentence as she read aloud. She sat back against the battered leather chair and attempted to cover her bare toes with the hem of her flannel pajamas. With another shiver coursing through her, Mairin inched her chair closer to the fire and opened the frayed green book, cracking the old spine audibly.

Mairin flicked the pages until she found a song she knew — *The First Nowell*. She chuckled at the antiquated spelling, and took another long pull of hot chocolate. Then she put the mug down and hummed the song, slowly waving the book around like a conductor's baton. Halfway through the second verse, a thin notebook slid out of the book and landed in her lap.

Mairin held the yellowed pages to her nose and deeply inhaled the mustiness — the scent of a church. She opened the notebook to the first page and admired the bold, rakish loops of handwriting, composed in a seasonal shade of deep green ink.

NDG Christmas Bird Census, M.N. was written across the top of the lined paper, with the years 1905 to 1930 inscribed down the left margin. Mairin perked up.

"What the ... crazy."

She ran her finger over the words, incredulous.

"M.N.? That must be Grandpa Murray. He was a bird fancier too? Far out," Mairin mumbled under her breath.

Dec 25, 1905. Villa Maria school. 14 degrees F, overcast. Deep snow, 2 feet. 2 Downy Woodp. 2 WB nuthatch. 1 Crow.

Villa! That's just up the street! Mairin took a long swig of hot chocolate, spilling some. She wiped her chin with the back of her sleeve and continued reading, with the soles of her feet propped up by the fire.

Dec 25, 1906. Villa Maria sch. -4 F, heavy snow, deep, 3 feet with thin ice crust. SCREWY COLD WINTER. 1 Downy Woodp., 3 WB nuthatch, 2 SNOWBIRD? Albino Redpoll or Snow Bunting? Smaller than Robin. See notes.

After this entry, Mairin's grandfather Murray Nolan had made two small but detailed drawings in the right-hand margin, both depicting an all-white bird with a black bill. The bird had a graceful, elongated body profile, with long wings and a horizontal stance. It looked to Mairin's eyes like a Snow Bunting with the crest of a Northern Cardinal. She knew that Snow Buntings preferred arctic tundra. They were rarely seen as far south as Montréal, while Northern Cardinals were strictly American birds, and had only been recorded a handful of times in Québec. However, according to a local researcher, they were thought to be expanding their range northwards.

"Snowbird? What's a Snowbird?"

Under that entry, there was a gap of blank rows, into which

the years between 1915 and 1923 had apparently disappeared. Mairin squinted at the entries after 1923, which were penned in a different hand, surely not by the same person who had started the list. The later entries were terse, and written in a pale, spidery scrawl that was hard to read in spots.

With Mairin hunched over the pages in deep concentration, her mother Elaine came into the room holding her own mug of hot chocolate.

"It's beginning to look a lot like Christmas, eh Mair? Everything OK? I heard things falling in here," Elaine said.

Mairin glanced at the mug and thought, *Good, she should be in a good mood when I tell her I'm thinking about dropping out.*

"Yeah Ma, I was just looking at some old books," Mairin said.

"I see. So good to have you back, and at this time of year. Have I said that yet? Yes I have. You're too close to the fire with that chair. Don't," she looked down into her mug — "fall asleep there, or you'll wake up on fire."

Mairin rolled her eyes and smiled.

Elaine stood behind the lounger and ruffled a hand through her daughter's hair, which had been cropped into a bob.

"Why did you do this to your pretty hair, Mair? Oof, it looks kind of silly."

"Yeah, yeah. Aaaah, shadapppp ..."

Elaine laughed, then reached for *Christmas Carols, New and Old.*

"What do you have there? Ah, I remember this book. We sang carols out of this when I was younger than you are now."

Mairin held the notebook up for her mother's inspection.

"This was in there too. You never told me Grandpa Murray was also a bird fancier. He was doing Christmas Bird Counts, Ma, like I am this year! And we're both counting in NDG — he was doing it up at Villa. What are the odds, eh Ma? I flipped my lid when I saw this, ain't that crazy? And there are some weird things in here I have to figure out, some weird white Snowbirds. A Christmas mystery!"

"Yes, I guess your love of birds runs in the family. Your grandfather Murray went out and counted the birds every Christmas, Mom said. No matter the weather. And he travelled quite a bit for work, so he was always looking for new birds in his spare time, like you. Is that Christmas count for your ... little club at school there?"

"Yeah, Ma, we're the Bishop's University Bird Appreciation Society. I'm the only girl. We each get a different part of the province to count birds in on Christmas Day, and I'm gonna count up around here, in NDG. Way back in the moldy oldie days, they used to do a hunt on Christmas Day, where two teams would try to blast more birds than the other. Great Christmas, huh? Creaming birds with a shotgun? And a partridge in a BLAM-O!"

Mairin slammed her hand on the side table and shouted for effect, louder than she meant to, making her mother flinch.

"Sorry, Ma. So this guy started a bird counting contest on Christmas instead, in 1900. An American guy, Chaplain, I think. Because killing all the birds on Christmas was lame, totally square."

"I see, so it's become a contest now?"

"Yeah, Ma, sort of."

Mairin pointed to the first page of the notebook.

"Hey, why wasn't Grandpa Murray doing the bird census from 1915 to 1923?"

Elaine held up the pages but looked past them at the tree for a long moment, then handed them back with a sigh.

"Well, Dad went over to France and fought in the Great War. Only came back in 1919, after getting very sick. It's ... it's like what your father went through after his war. Understand, hun?"

"Elvis came out of the army alright," Mairin said, taking another bright-eyed sip from her mug.

Elaine folded her arms.

"Elvis wasn't a real soldier. Elvis didn't have to go to war, Mair. War changes whoever's in it. Kills them ... on the inside, in a way. Anyway, this is hardly a cheerful holiday conversation."

She handed her daughter two long candy-striped wool socks she had draped over her shoulder. "See what I found in a box? The old Christmas stockings you made when you were in Madame Morissette's class. Grade three was it?"

Mairin nodded, then rubbed the socks across her cheek and beamed.

"Thanks Ma, you really are groovy. They will come in handy. It's really ... it's a *screwy cold winter*, isn't it?"

Elaine gave Mairin an odd look.

"Yes, a *screwy cold winter*. Groovy? OK, I'm assuming that's good?"

"Yes Maaaa, you're the real living end."

The two shared another laugh, then the elder Lang stood up and clinked her mug to her daughter's.

"Great to have you back, Mair. Merry Christmas," Elaine said, then mussed her daughter's hair again.

"Time to check back on the oven. Have fun with your little Christmas mystery, but don't get too wrapped up in it. Your grandfather was a little bit ... different. Even before the war," Elaine said as she stood up and headed towards the kitchen.

"... and so are you," she said under her breath, glancing back.

Mairin inched the socks onto her icy feet and smiled. She stroked her grandfather's words on the pages and finished her hot chocolate, to the snapping of the fire.

"Snowbirds, snowbiiiiiirds," she hummed, to the tune of *The First Noel*, and closed her eyes as the fire waned to dark orange embers.

"What do you have there? Ah, I remember this book. We sang carols out of this when I was younger than you are now."

CHAPTER 2

December 17, 1960

Mairin was up early, bundled on the couch in the dull light of a winter dawn. She was slouched over her grandfather's notes on the coffee table by the Christmas tree, drinking tea.

The brittle pages that came after Grandfather Murray's main Christmas lists contained more detailed notes about specific sightings, with the bulk of them pertaining to the enigmatic 'Snowbirds' he had sighted on the grounds of the nearby Villa Maria School. Murray Nolan had been a meticulous note-taker with a knack for recording the details that mattered — especially impressive considering that he had barely entered his teenage years when his Christmas bird census efforts began.

Dec 25, 1906. Villa Maria sch. -4 degrees F. Observed Snowbirds again at apple rocks. Two birds — a pair? How to fig. if ♂ or ♀? Not in any book. Black eyes and legs, rules out albinos? Alb. should have red eyes, pink legs. Maybe all-white Snow Bunting subspecies — body seems same shape. Curious call: piercing, rising double rasp. Some odd snow-pokeys in the ice crust near rocks.

Mairin flipped back to the first page again, and studied it with a frown, while absent-mindedly chewing on her hair again. After the first sightings in 1906, her grandfather had recorded sightings of the Snowbirds in only two other years — 1914 and 1925.

Dec 25, 1914. Villa Maria. -2 degrees F. Another Screwy Cold Winter. Thin ice crust on 4 feet of snow, hard going on the hill. Snowbird back at AR, what a surprise. Only one. Same peculiar call, and holes in the ice.

9

Dec 25, 1925. V.M. SCW again. Ice. 4 S.Birds. Saw them make a snow-pokey.

Mairin spat out her hair and pushed back from the coffee table.

"Unreal. Three screwy cold winters, three Snowbird sightings at Villa. AR? Apple Rocks! But what is a snow-pokey?"

A faint inscription in the margin at the bottom of the 1925 entry caught her eye.

Lovely Christmas. A ham for dinner. All the uncles came over. Bought wee Elaine (5) a doll for Christmas. She threw it down and asked for a nicer one.

"Ha! I feel ya, Murray, she's the same today."

"Who are you talking to in here?" Elaine tisked as she approached the narrow living room.

Mairin laughed and waved a page of notes at her mother, "... I was talking to good ol' Murray, the bird man of NDG."

"Hmmm," Elaine said, donning a frayed wool coat.

"Hey Ma, what did Grandpa look like? I don't think I've seen pictures of him."

"Oh you must have, before the move, surely. There are some pictures of him I can show you, just not right now. I still haven't unpacked them. He was handsome, your grandfather."

"OK. Hey, I may go to McGill University."

"Oh wow, Mair, that would be such a step up. But I thought

your grades — "

"Ma, no, I mean later in the week. I think I still have a friend of a friend in the Climatology Department there. I gotta pick his brain about some screwy cold winters."

"Oh, sorry, I — "

"Yeah yeah, Ma, wicked. Go do your shopping already. Hit the road!"

"You sure you don't need anything from downtown? I'll be at the Hudson's Bay."

"No Ma, I just need some apple rocks and a snow-pokey to put my Snowbirds in, alright-ee-o?"

"Strange child. Wear a slicker, it looks like sleet out there. Don't fall and twist an ankle."

Mairin put on a husky Chubby Checker voice and jumped up. She came at her mother, dancing and swaying menacingly.

"A slicker? OK, I'm Chubby Slicker, and I'm gonna come tw-tw-TWIST your ankle!"

Elaine made a swatting motion at her daughter, as if she were a mosquito.

"Come on baybehhhh, let's do-ah the twist-ahhh!"

Elaine put her palm over her daughter's face and shoved her away gently.

"Bye, Mair, my loony daughter," Elaine sighed, then pulled on her gloves and headed down the narrow stairs of the upstairs duplex.

Mairin stood up.

"Well, time to go to Villa Maria, scope it all out and find those apple rocks. We'll see what Grandpa was talking about with his Snowbirds."

CHAPTER 3

"Now this," Mairin expelled a puff of icy breath, "... is a screwy cold winter, sure as God made little green apples," she hissed through teeth that felt like iced Chiclets. The wind was carving in horizontally, carrying with it microscopic blades of ice that stung the young woman's exposed face and hands.

Perhaps because the grounds of the Villa Maria school lay only a few blocks from Mairin's family home, she was woefully underdressed. Mairin wore canvas Keds runners over her striped grade three socks, all of which had soaked through with melted snow. She got to the top of a long side street that had been plowed and stood at Villa Maria's back gates, in front of a ledge of snow that reached the tops of her shins.

"Sheesh, guess they forgot to plow in here. OK, so this place is huge. Where are the apple rocks? And more importantly, what are the apple rocks?"

Like a hesitant horse, Mairin lifted one leg and pushed it down through the ice-crusted snow. The snow was up to her knees. She paused in thought, scanning the massive white soccer fields, then the hills behind the hundred-year-old buildings that had long served as a nunnery before being converted into a school for rich girls. Mairin did not hear the man approach from behind her, and his thin voice made her jump.

"You OK, miss?"

"Yeah. Yes. Yes, thank you. I'm, um, looking for birds. Just counting birds for a Christmas bird census thingy," Mairin blurted.

This was met with a blank look from the man, who was perhaps in his 60s. He held a wide shovel and was dressed for the weather, with high rubbered galoshes belted up below his knees, and a wool trench coat. His weathered, smiling face was framed by a fur flap-hat.

"I'm in a bird club. At my university."

"OK, miss, well that's fine, but please be careful. You'll get up to here if you go off the trails," the man held his hand up to his waist, then looked up into the purpling sky. "... and there's a heavy snow and more ice coming, a blizzard maybe. You don't want to be getting lost in there, OK? Stick to those footprints there; they're mine. The snow is compact there, but on either side, you'll go right through."

"OK, I'm OK, thanks," Mairin said, but her uncertainty soaked through her voice.

The man took her bare hand in his, and spoke with a familiar warmth.

"Well you'll figure it out, I'm sure, Mairin. Au revoir."

A stranger taking her hand would normally have creeped Mairin out, but the man exuded a calmness, a goodness she absorbed, without registering it. His hand was warm and leathery.

"Sure thing. Oh hey wait, are there ... apple rocks here?"

"Apple rocks? Huh. Well, the old orchard is up there," he said, pointing to a small hill thickly laced with bony sumac limbs, "... still some apple trees there, but be careful of that crumbly cliff face. And there are a couple of sunken building foundations there, too. Don't fall in 'em."

"Apple orchard? That could be the spot. What were the

foundations for? Old church or something?"

"Nope, they're called the Gall ruins, 'bout 50–60 years old or thereabouts. Not sure what they were, really, but they didn't build 'em well, that's for sure."

"Thanks, mister."

"Sure thing. Remember, you watch out for that screwy weather coming in tonight. Should be icy 'til well past Christmas. And call me Cob. I'll be here all through the holidays if you need anything."

"Thanks, Cob."

Wait, did I tell him my name? Mairin thought as the man walked back down the path, but the notion was swept away by her restless mind, as she barged her way up through hip-deep snow, using sumac limbs for support. The sunken foundations Cob had mentioned were covered in an icing of thick, unbroken snow.

After a ten-minute slog, Mairin was huffing by the time she crested the hill, but she did not register the cold's bite on her feet and ankles anymore. She had made it up the vaunted hill, and, in spite of the cold, saw that the area was gorgeous — an oasis of quiet, snowy fields and woods, surrounded by the faraway lights of a growing neighbourhood.

Mairin punched and brushed the ice and snow off a section of odd purplish rocks that stood out somehow. The upwelling of jagged rocks did not seem to belong in the middle of Montréal.

"The Arctic, more like it," Mairin whispered, as she examined the frozen lichens she had exposed from under the snow. There were several bare fruit trees atop the hill.

Most likely apple trees ... this must be the spot. Apple rocks. Murray did mention a hill, and yes, it was hard going.

Closer to the rocks, there were trees of a much different sort that got Mairin's attention. Mairin had never seen anything like the stunted, crooked conifers before in person, even in her *Intro to Botany* class. *Almost like those little trees in Japan.* She had seen similar examples of wind-gnarled arctic trees in textbooks, however — *krummholz trees.* As she ran the tips of her chilled fingers across the bark of one of the odd trees, they touched metal.

"Hello, what's this?"

A metal name placard, heavily dimpled with age, was secured around the trunk of the tree. There was a stout wrought-iron frame around the square tag, wrapped around the tree with a thin chain that had been half-absorbed by the growing bark around it. Mairin leaned close to read it by the light of the waning moon.

"Ferrr ... ias dersuensis? Ferias dersuensis."

Mairin turned the small metal tag over in her hand absent-mindedly and repeated the plant's scientific name several times to commit it to memory. She touched the letters, which were weathered smooth, and almost illegible.

"Wow, this thing must be as old as the pyramids. Far out."

She looked back down the hill at the sunken foundations, then at the skeletal remains of two tiny Victorian greenhouses that huddled nearby on the hill. Shaped like oversized round-topped bird cages, not a single pane of glass remained intact.

What did Cob say? The ruins ... the Gall ruins. Check that later too, Mair. The Gall ruins, the Gall ruins, Ferias dersuensis,

Ferias dersuensis.

Mairin frowned down at several fist-sized holes that perforated the ice crust under some of the tiny trees, and kicked at one lightly.

Chirrup-ruuuup!

Something burst from the snow nearby in a wisp of white powder.

Mairin snapped her head to the left, and felt the roots of her hair prickling to attention under her hat.

Chirrup-rup-ruuuup!

A smudge of motion in her periphery, white on white, clipped past too quickly for Mairin to follow. Mairin then sensed she was again alone on the hill, and released a breath she did not remember holding.

"Holy smokes!"

She imitated the call she had heard, to keep it fresh in her memory.

"Chirrup! Ruuup! A piercing ... *Chiruupruuup* ... double rasp, yessireebob. Far, far out. I found your bird, Murray. I found your Snowbird. Chiruupruuuup!"

Mairin looked up at the knuckles of vertical rocks above her, which were topped with more of the diminutive trees, and shook her head.

"Not tonight," she laughed, then turned on her heel and took in her picture postcard surroundings for a long moment.

Mairin rubbed her hands together and blew on them to regain some sensation, then slid and high-stepped back down the hill towards home with her hands wedged into her armpits.

Upon returning home, Mairin threw her jacket down, picked up Murray's notes, and went straight to her spot by the fire.

January 8, 1926
Took my Snowbird sightings to Dr. Drouin at McGill Univ. He dismissed the whole concept of the Snowbird outright. What does he know anyway, just an empty suit.

Towards the end of the notebook, following a section of pages that had been torn out, there were several pages of notes that started under the heading: ***Abstract: Projected north-ern territorial expansion of Northern Cardinal.***

The notes were written in the same prose and handwriting as Murray's prewar writings — deep, animated strokes. All at once, Mairin realized that both vintages of handwriting had been written by her grandfather, with the weak postwar scrawls hinting at a much-diminished man.

"Abstract? Geez, Murray was writing a thesis!"

Mairin skimmed the abstract for highlights.

In summary, it seems that the Northern Cardinal is not a resident species as commonly thought, but one that is actively expanding its range to the north in reaction perhaps to environmental stressors. This expansion is probably taking place in fits and starts on narrow salients, making it problematic to observe and record unless and until a wider network of bird observations exists. Perhaps as Christmas bird censuses increase in scope and popularity, the raw data recorded by these citizen counters could be utilized to build a much wider picture of the actual distribution patterns of the Northern Cardinal, and other species, which I feel are in constant evolution as various species react to the changing environment and opportunities around them.

In the margins, Murray had written: *Possible same thing happening with the Snowbirds but in the opposite direction?*

"Boy, were you ever ahead of your age, Murray," Mairin marveled, then turned to a later entry.

September 24, 1928

Took my findings on Northern Cardinals to Drouin again, he was very interested this time. Worked with him for three weeks, going over some of my findings, but not all of them. Then one fine day, he wouldn't return my calls and it seems the rat published his PhD thesis on guess what ... the projected northward wanderings of the Northern Cardinal! Drouin stole my work, but how to prove it? Too tired to fight him on it. Where's the use in it?

The pen-strokes were especially deep when they spelled out the words 'Dr. Drouin.' Small ink splatters were evident around the last instance of his name, like Murray had stabbed at it in anger with the fountain pen.

Mairin flipped the pages of the notebook to the end, but was disappointed when she did not find any of the hard data her grandfather had gathered on Northern Cardinals during his business travels — the data that could prove that Dr. Drouin's thesis in fact had originally been her grandfather's breakthrough.

Mairin closed the notebook and set it down.

"Oh boy, Murray, another mystery? First things first. Let's figure out our Snowbird."

Chirrup-rup-ruuuup!

CHAPTER 4

December 23, 1960

After a 30-minute ride on a foggy-windowed bus along Sherbrooke Street, Mairin got off at McGill University and made the trek up through the picturesque campus towards the science buildings.

The Botany Department was already locked up for the holidays, but after a quick trip to the library, Mairin found her Ferias dersuensis tree in a massive book with lush colour plates. Ferias dersuensis was a rare subspecies of dwarf spruce, found only in the high Arctic of the Canadian Shield. The tree was notable for its extensive root system, and for producing small edible brown berries near the base of its trunk through the harshest of winters.

Mairin found the History Department also shut, so she cursed and slogged back to the library. With some help from a librarian, she found an article on microfilm about Gall from *The Montréal Gazette*, from January of 1897, titled: "Alasdair Gall's 'Arctic World' Bid to Compete with World's Fair a Flop."

Mairin read about the grandiose plan that Gall, a Scottish grifter, had pitched to the Montréal mayor's office. He sketched out his plans for "Artic World," an outdoor museum and zoo of sorts, which would supposedly put Montréal on the map in the same manner that the World's Fair of 1896 had done for Chicago. The quaint grounds of the Villa Maria school were set as the unlikely location for the grandiose exposition. Gall's plan, authorities speculate, was to fleece three levels of government, as well as wealthy local investors, then blow town and vanish somewhere abroad.

Gall billed it as a sort of World's Fair in miniature, and had prepared some quite ambitious conceptual drawings, but in the end it was all found to be bunk. When the time came to showcase the site to the press, potential investors, and officials from the mayor's office, all Gall had managed to set up on the grounds of Villa Maria were several small, unfinished buildings, two miniature greenhouses containing 'exotic arctic flora,' six plywood polar bears, and two supposed "Eskimos" in seal skins, who were thought to have been actors.

Mairin scrolled through the article and took notes with an excited hand.

Mairin went up a flight of stairs and poked her head into the Climatology Department. Her appearance straightened up a sleepy old Englishman with unruly wisps of cumulonimbus hair who had been half-slumped over a mound of paperwork. The office had a noticeable mustiness to it — a comforting blend of damp mushrooms and old books.

"Professor Nash? I'm Mairin Lang. I'm a friend of Dr. Zerafa over at Bishop's, he gave me your name. I was hoping I could pick your brain about something for a few minutes."

"Yes, hello, come on in. You're lucky anyone is here. Today is the last day of office hours. You've caught me in the middle of grading some papers. Well, in the middle of a break from grading papers, as it were. Here, have a seat please," he said, shoving a stack of newspapers off a chair with one hand, and making a vain effort to tamp down his wild locks with the other.

"Thank you so much, Professor. I'll try to make it quick, and let you get back to it."

Mairin smiled at the old professor's bumbling, cheerful demeanour. She pulled a folded scrap of paper from her pocket and flattened it out in front of him.

Screwy cold winters, was written at the top of the paper, and under that were four years.

1905, 1914, 1925 ... 1960?

"Screwy cold winters, eh? May I ... may I ask your question for you before you do?" the professor said with a sparkle, and sat up a bit straighter.

"Sure," Mairin said.

"Your screwy cold winters, these years ... well they're well-known to us in this department. These years all featured winters with above-average precipitation combined with below-average temperatures in this part of the world. This is all down to warm ocean currents coming up from the equatorial region, you see. Electronic ocean probes gather that data now, would you believe, all very fancy gear, that. In these screwy years here, it will be drier than normal out west, but here in the northeast it's wet and cold in the winter. Happens once or twice a decade, to varying degrees. And to answer your '1960?' question ... yes, we are having one this year, as you may have noticed," Professor Nash said, jabbing his hand towards the howling whiteness on the other side of his iced window.

"OK, great. And what about up north? In the Arctic? What happens there during these screwy cold winters?" Mairin asked.

"Ah, excellent question. And one that has no satisfactory answer yet, as it is a lot easier to convince grad students to go down to the tropics for their fieldwork than is the case for the high Arctic, you see? Would you be interested at all in doing a few months up there in a tent?" he said with a chuckle. Mairin smiled and shook her head with a mock shiver.

"In any case, I suspect that the situation in the Arctic in these abnormal years would lead perhaps to uneven heat and cold cycles, which would alter the normal snow and ice patterns."

"What would this do to the animals, the birds and stuff, up there?" Mairin said.

"Well I imagine it would be quite disconcerting for them, really. Disruptive to normal feeding and breeding. Icing and melting coming at all the wrong moments. Would lead to phenomena such as an unexpected loss of sea ice, or conversely, conditions that bring about abnormal icing events. But that's just an old climatologist having a guess, eh?"

"Thank you so much for your time, Professor Nash. Merry Christmas," Mairin said.

"Merry Christmas, dear. Do give my best to Dr. Zerafa if you would, please."

Mairin's final research stop brought her to the cramped biology labs hidden behind the wood paneling in the Redpath Museum. As Mairin reached up to touch the tail of a massive dinosaur skeleton, the museum's centerpiece, a grad student with a dark three-day scruff rounded a corner and waved his hands high to gain her attention.

"Hey, hi, sorry, don't touch it."

Mairin withdrew her hand.

"Thanks. We don't touch the dinosaur. You must be Miss Lang, right? Zerafa told me you'd be coming by today. You're in the Bishop's University Bird Appreciation Society?" he said, managing to be both pushy and shy. Mairin sized him up and picked up a not-so-subtle vibe that he was sweet on her.

"Yes, that's right. And that would make you Rodney Arnold, right? Zerafa told me you guys were in high school together back in Vermont."

After they had settled into Rodney's tiny office and exchanged pleasantries, Mairin showed Rodney her grandfather's drawings of a Snowbird. The young academic frowned and tilted his head at the picture.

"Well, it's got the morphology of a Snow Bunting. Not sure why it's all white, or what the crest is about. Was your grandfather an artist? Just making something up? Because this isn't a real species he drew," Rodney scoffed.

Mairin scrunched her eyebrows together.

"My grandfather was a serious bird-fancier. He participated in some of the very first Christmas Bird Counts in Canada ... the first to do it in NDG, and that was when he was about 13 years old."

Rodney let out a pained sigh, but tried to hide it with a smile. He touched Mairin's sleeve.

"So Mairin, I know your grandfather was probably a great birdwatcher, but do you think that when he drew this ... I mean he was just a kid ... that it represents a real bird?"

"Alright, let's change the tune for a minute, Rodney. Does Dr. Drouin still work here? Seems my grandfather came to him when he first found his bird. Our bird. It seems like Dr.

Drouin gave him a similar reception to the one you just gave me," Mairin said with a mischievous sneer.

Rodney's demeanour suddenly grew somber.

"I had the pleasure of meeting Dr. Drouin once, but I never studied under him. He was drummed out of the department because of the ... the proclivities of his private life, but we're all still quite proud of him, and defensive of what he achieved here. He put our department on the map."

"Yes, his study on Northern Cardinals. I read about it, that was the big one for him, wasn't it? His research all checks out?" Mairin said, leaning in.

"Yes. Well, besides the fact that his initial migration data was a bit on the thin side, the rest of his hypotheses and findings all worked out in the end. A groundbreaking study, as was his suggestion about using Christmas Bird Counts to augment scientifically-gathered migration and demographic data."

"Hmmm," Mairin said, her tone skeptical.

"And if Dr. Drouin thought your grandfather's Snowbirds were bunk, then they're bunk," he said with a weak smile. "Sorry."

"They're not bunk. I think I heard one too, in the same place. A couple of days ago in NDG."

Rodney squinted.

"You *heard* it. What did it sound like?"

"I dunno. Like ... like he described it. Like this: *Chiruuup-rup!*"

Rodney's eyebrows furrowed. He looked back at the drawing and shook his head.

"Alright. Just humour me for a bit here," Mairin said, taking back the drawing.

"What if someone brought some birds down here from the Arctic? Maybe to put in a zoo or an exhibit or something, and they got loose?"

"Why would someone even do that? I mean look, the McKay's Bunting, which is similar to the Snow Bunting, there *is* a population way up in Alaska. But they have black primary feathers on their wings. You're talking about an all-white bird here. That's going to be an albino. And with the crest in that picture, that's not a real bird, like I said. Just a fantasy. A pretty drawing."

"But he had no reason to make it up. He never told anyone."

Rodney shrugged, and Mairin thought she saw him smirk too.

"Never told anyone but Dr. Drouin?"

The back of Mairin's neck started to get hot. She took a deep breath.

"Alright let's just say, hypothetically, that these birds do exist in the Arctic. Why would they come this far south? Would weird weather make them come down here in some winters? Say, in a year like this one, when the tropical currents mess with our weather up here, and make it colder and wetter than normal?"

Rodney arched an eyebrow.

"Aha, now we're getting into something more interesting.

Hard science. I actually teach a module on what you're describing. Sometimes northern birds do end up getting displaced from their normal ranges."

"Interesting. And could they have been on the move because of that abnormal weather?" Mairin said.

"Yes, of course, I was getting to that. Species like owls and finches will sometimes come down as far as Montréal, and sometimes even well south down into the States in some winters, because the weather conditions make it miserable for them where they normally live, in the high Arctic."

"Like what? Miserable like how?"

Rodney looked up, frowning, trying to retrieve an elusive fact.

"Well, the ... the owls come down when the weather heats up in mid-winter, I believe. The lemmings and other prey species they depend on can hide under the coating of ice on the snow. The owls can't get at them. And the finches, like the Crossbills and Redpolls — "

"I know finches," Mairin said with a toss of her head that came off as more defensive than she had intended.

"Yes, so the finches will roam down south when their pine cone crops have a bad year, due to a rough spring."

"How often does stuff like that happen? Arctic birds coming down this far south?"

"Oh, maybe once or twice a decade. This is an area that is only just starting to be studied — abnormal seasonal movements due to adverse climatological factors. But they can also get lost when they're migrating, pushed by a storm, for instance. Or sometimes a bird will abmigrate, which is where they're migrating in the wrong direction."

"And what if one of these roaming or abmigrating birds from the north finds a little slice of home here? Like a little bunch of arctic trees and berries it likes?"

"Arctic trees? I don't know about that, but yes, it is possible for a misplaced bird to settle in say, an arboretum, where it finds some trees from its native area and gets confused. It's happened in Florida a few times, in an arboretum down there. Some type of dove I think."

"Are there any birds that feed on the berries of the Ferias dersuensis tree?"

"Ferias dersuensis? I don't know."

Rodney wrinkled his nose.

"OK, thanks Rodney, you've been a tremendous help."

"Sure thing. Hey, will you let me know if you find anything else? I don't think it's anything, but it could be quite an exciting find if it's not just some albino. If you discovered an unknown species, you'd be in the newspaper, I imagine."

"Huh, I thought you said it was fantasy."

Rodney shrugged and mumbled: "So yeah, I mean you can stop by here any time you want. If you wanted to ... to maybe talk more about birds I mean."

Mairin noticed his face had gone a shade pinker.

"Alright. Have yourself a merry little Christmas, Roddy-o!" Mairin sang as she skipped out of the office. She went out of her way to touch the dinosaur on the way out.

"Hey, hi, sorry, don't touch it."

CHAPTER 5

Mairin twisted the pieces of the avian riddle into place on the bus ride back to her neighbourhood, Notre-Dame-de-Grâce, trying to construct a narrative that made sense.

Think, Mair! So ... in 1896, that Gall guy somehow got a bunch of Ferias dersuensis trees from the Arctic and tried to use them as part of his big Arctic World con, which flopped. But ... the trees stayed at Villa Maria. Ten years later, and in those other weird winters, the weather up in the Arctic forced a species of all-white birds, Snowbirds, to roam south in search of greener pastures, and some of them found Gall's trees. And then, in a holiday miracle, my Grandpa Murray found the Snowbirds while helping out with one of Canada's first Christmas bird counts, just six blocks from his home. It's all too crazy to be real. No, it's real alright. But what are they? They're not albinos ... a totally new species of bunting after all? A Crested Snow Bunting?

The bus driver's announcement snapped Mairin from her deductive reverie. She got off the bus at its final stop, Monkland and Décarie, and hopped over a towering snow bank to get to the sidewalk. She had hoped to get to Villa Maria before the sun went down, but the brick-dust orange horizon told her she had lingered too long at McGill.

Despite being better prepared, Mairin's rubber boots still managed to let some snow in as she pressed on. This time though, her feet were not totally drenched. She stamped a meandering row of footprints through the sheet of ice covering the deep snow, an attempt to make her passage easier.

When she reached the rocky area where the mockup for Arctic World had once stood, Mairin pushed past the sumac and apple trees, then powered up and around a hill with a gentler grade. She then pulled herself to the top of the small plateau that stood twenty feet above where she had found the metal tree tag.

There were about fifteen of the gnarled trees hunched at the top, with several of the odd holes interspersed between them. Mairin crouched and inspected one of the holes. It started where the odd brown berries clustered, and seemed to tunnel down into a labyrinth of roots, like a frozen rabbit warren.

"Looks like Swiss cheese, wicked. Are these the snow-pokeys? Time for a stakeout."

Mairin pushed closer to the edge of the cliff and clung to one of the Ferias dersuensis trees with both hands. She wedged the toe of her left boot into a small orifice in the crumbly cliff face for stability, then peered along the undulating surface of the snow.

For twenty minutes, nothing moved but paisleys of ice crystals blowing off a nearby roof, twisting down in shimmering ribbons that lashed at Mairin's face. To Mairin, it felt like three hours had passed, as the blood in her immobile extremities began to retreat towards her core, causing her fingers and toes to tingle with frostbite's early grumblings.

She began contemplating making a strategic retreat when a squadron of five American Crows dipped low overhead and landed in a tall poplar. The corvids perched silently, heads twisting this way and that as they scrutinized the holes in the snow for a long moment, before departing en masse with a single caw from the lead bird.

Their departure provoked the sort of fantastic series of events Mairin had envisioned since she had discovered her grandfather's Christmas bird diary. From the ridge above the small plateau that Mairin clung to, a puff of snow flowered, and a white blur flew towards the Ferias dersuensis trees. The young birdwatcher's bottom jaw popped open as an elegant, all-white bird flew straight at her on a serpentine trajectory. It deployed its long white wings like a parachute an instant before landing on one of the small trees, slowing itself to a hover and alighting on a low branch in slow-motion.

From fifteen feet away, Mairin took in the exquisite, streamlined bird. It had swept-back wings that displayed an effortless speed, even at a standstill. It was a pure white, save for the tiny black eyes, nub bill, and feet, just as Murray had described it.

Looks like a pricey Christmas ornament from the Hudson's Bay. No, like a hood ornament on one of those old fancy cars.

Mairin took the bird in for several long minutes. It pecked at the brown berries with its tiny bill and scanned warily; its crest mostly tucked flat. It was perfectly camouflaged on the branch, looking just like a skiff of snow. The caw of a distant crow broke the moment.

The white bird twitched, extended its small crest, then hurled itself off the branch. Wings tight against its flanks, it dropped straight down like a lawn dart. The bird landed hard on the snow and stilled, rendering itself invisible. Mairin squinted in disbelief.

She fished her Leica 8x30 binoculars from her pocket and focused on the patch of snow where the bird had landed for several minutes, but still could not locate it. Mairin pivoted her anchor foot to get a better angle, cracking off several slices of the small rock shelf that were supporting her weight in the process.

Nothing ... nothing ... did it fly off? Nothing ... there? There!

Mairin saw a patch of snow ripple almost imperceptibly, and realized that the bird had driven itself under the ice crust, leaving only its tail tip and head peeking out. She could faintly make out one tiny black eye, surveying for hostile shapes in the black-blue sky of the gloaming.

The white bird poked its head out a bit further. The snow on its back quivered as the bird ruffled and shook its way up through the snow. It hopped cautiously across the ice, still almost completely invisible. Once it was certain there were no further threats afoot, the bird darted in low flight along the ice-capped snow. It landed at the base of another Ferias dersuensis tree and again vanished, perhaps into one of the holes above the tree's roots.

Wowwww.

Mairin had never heard of a songbird engaging in that type of snow-burying behaviour when it came to defensive camouflage. Sure, some grouse species roosted under the snow at night, but *hiding* in the snow? *Fantastic! How could it know to do that, to hide itself in white snow like that, if it was an albino bird? Is that sort of thing a learned behaviour?* Mairin's thoughts were a disorganized swarm.

She watched the area with the mysterious Swiss cheese holes for several more minutes, her mind again ignoring the frostbite alerts her body broadcasted. The last thing Mairin saw before her world went sideways was the Snowbird pull itself free from the snow in the distance, and offer spectacular side views through the frost-flecked lenses of her binoculars. Straining to see the bird, she twisted her foot and stood on her toes, causing the final shard of rock

34

holding her to crack and crumble away.

As Mairin fell back, she grabbed the spindly trunk of one of the dwarf spruces and watched as the roots wrenched free from the snow. She looked calmly at the roots and snow clods spinning in slow motion against the black sky. Mairin's stomach dropped as she crashed down the 20-foot cliff, a tangle of reflexively flailing limbs. She landed hard on her ankle against the base of the cliff then fell through the ice crust, sending sparks of red pain darting through her system. Her mind went silent with a final flash.

Mairin came to in the dark, a veil of snow covering her face. The cold, combined with the pain in her ankle, tormented her into consciousness. She squawked and writhed her head free from the snow, her face wet with tears and melted snow. Mairin propped herself up on her elbows and tried to stand. A fresh spear of pain from her ankle knocked her back. The wind picked up with a snarling vengeance, and Mairin pulled her head back beneath the level of the ice crust with a whimper, protecting herself as the Snowbird had done. She became vaguely aware that she had lost a boot in the fall, as well as a mitten.

The first icy tendrils of panic slid into Mairin's mind at the same time as the involuntary shivering began from somewhere deep inside of her. She tried again to stand up, but she was anticipating the ankle pain with dread this time, and flinched and flopped back down at the first sign of it.

Am I really going to die? I'm too young. I'm only six blocks from home, and my mother will never know what happened to me. I haven't told her I'm dropping out and I haven't wrapped her presents yet.

Mairin tried to crawl through the ice-covered snow and got

about fifteen feet before she collapsed again, her chin and bottom lip bloodied from repeatedly breaking through the ice. She was spent, and the adrenaline sloshing through her made her feel colder and rawer than she had ever felt. She closed her eyes.

Am I really going to die right before Christmas?

"No, you aren't, miss," the man said, and lifted Mairin into a seated position by her lapels.

"Ummff. Whuuu?" Mairin groaned.

The man pinched her cheeks sharply, waking her up by a degree. Mairin winced.

"What? I'm in ... Cob?"

"That's right, miss. Are you OK? This is no place for a nap," Cob said without a hint of humour.

"Why ... how long ... here? I'm cold."

"Long enough. You asked me if you were going to die on Christmas, and there'll be none of that. What are you doing here climbing the rocks on your own at night? And in this weather? Surely there are no birds to count for your club right now?"

Mairin rubbed her balled hands together and shook her head vigorously, to fend off the chill that had very nearly put her to rest for good.

"No. Yes. There um, there were crows. And the, one of the Snowbirds. White birds. Uhhh ... oh man ..."

The groundskeeper took his mitts off and held Mairin's hands together between his own. A billow of warmth — impossible warmth and vitality, passed into Mairin's hands and percolated through to the rest of her.

"The Snowbird. Where did it come from?" Cob whispered.

Mairin closed her eyes and let the warmth revive her body, which had been in the process of shutting down in surrender, one system at a time.

"Thank you," she said in a small voice.

Cob stood from his crouch and slowly helped Mairin to her feet. When she was standing, he swatted the snow off her pants by swinging his mittens.

Mairin took Cob's arm, then followed him gingerly through the rutted path he had forged in the deep snow, back towards the main trail to the Monkland street entrance. Mairin's words spilled out until she was out of breath.

"Thank you. So. The Snowbirds, I think, my theory, is that they're an unknown species of bunting from the Arctic that gets displaced by screwy weather every few years, and they found a special tree here, the Ferias dersuensis tree, that this guy Gall brought here. He was this con man, and the Snowbirds kind of get fooled by this tree and, because it reminds them of home, I guess, and they like the berries, and they roost under the snow, under the roots of the Ferias dersuensis tree."

"Ah. Under the roots, reminds them of home. So that explains it. So they're not albinos after all?"

"No, um, no. Not albinos," Mairin said with a curious head twist.

"It's just these screwy cold winters," the man laughed.

"Yes."

"Well this screwy cold winter almost took you, Mairin. I don't want to see you messing 'round in here at night, OK? I won't always be here to find you."

"Yes," Mairin said, still with a dreamy slur to her voice.

Cob held both of Mairin's hands and helped her hobble over the four-foot snow bank that lined the trail back down to Monkland. The two ambled down the path, and Mairin let the last of the significant shivers work their way through her. The old man handed Mairin her backpack and pinched her cheek again, this time more gently, in a familiar manner.

"Studia vestra sunt momenti, Mairin," Cob said in a voice so faint Mairin barely heard him.

"Excusez-moi?" Mairin replied, switching to French.

"I said, you go home and have Elaine make you some of her chicken rice soup, and put some hot water bottles on those toes and feet. Another 20 minutes and the frostbite would have set in for real. Could have lost some fingers. Have a warm drink. Sit by the fire."

"I ... thank you, Cob."

"Merry Christmas, Mairin," the old man said when they reached the main gate.

"Bye," Mairin said, "... Merry Christmas."

As she limped and squeezed through the gap in the gate, Mairin heard the raspy call of the Snowbird echo through the trees just for a second, before she stepped through to the street, and the wet swish of cars through slush washed the sound away.

Mairin looked down and saw her one rainbow-striped sock against the snow, and had a weak laugh. *You almost died, Mair, what's a stupid boot? Let's go warm up by the fire, dummy, like Cob said.*

Mairin's stomach dropped as she crashed down the 20-foot cliff,
a tangle of reflexively flailing limbs.

CHAPTER 6

December 24, 1960

On Christmas Eve, Mairin slept in until just after noon. She shuffled out into the living room, buried in her father's robe, and found her mother blowing a small fire to life in the fireplace. A mug steamed on the coffee table.

"Oh there's sleeping beauty. Thought you were going to sleep right through Christmas! There's some eggnog in the kitchen, shortbread cookies for breakfast too, because hey, 'tis the season. Here, you can have mine, I'll get some more in a bit," Elaine said, and handed the mug to Mairin, who had already cocooned herself onto the couch.

"You got in late last night," Mairin's mother said inquisitively, "... and you were into the hot water bottles."

"Uh-huh," Mairin replied, closing her eyes as she took a deep nip of her mother's eggnog, "... my feet got cold walking home from McGill; I missed the bus."

"Yeah, I saw your wet socks you left in a nice ball there. I put them on the radiator."

"Uh-huh," Mairin said, and took another sip, then pointed to the mug with her nose, "... s'good."

"Hey Mair, did you see your first gift? It's on the counter."

"The fruit cake? I saw that."

"I made you a whole one, just for you. You can eat it now, or take it back when you go back to school. It'll keep."

Mairin peered at her mother over the mug.

"Awww, thanks Ma. Hey, is it OK if I give it to a friend?"

"Sure, that's Christmas, right, gift-giving? As long as I get credit," she winked.

Mairin threw on her coat and walked the six blocks to Villa Maria in good time — the pain in her ankle had largely dimmed overnight, in spite of the vivid purple colour that had set in. The wan winter sun was out, warming the afternoon to a bearable -4°F. Mairin encountered a woman in a long grey jacket exiting Villa Maria as she was about to enter. The woman wore a hideous cat brooch. Mairin smiled and pointed up the long, tree-lined path to the school.

"Oh hi there, do you know if Cob is in there today?"

"Cob? I don't think so. Is that a student? No one at all here today, and I just came by to get something I forgot in my office."

"Cob the old ... the groundskeeper guy with the shovel. I've ... I brought him some fruitcake," Mairin held up the twine-wrapped butcher's paper bundle she carried.

The woman frowned in thought.

"Sorry dear, there's no groundskeeper here, not this winter. The city truck does our snow once a week, but no groundskeeper. The city has not come in nearly a week and a half actually, as you can see from the state of this path. And I am afraid there is no Cob on the staff, and I ought to know."

Mairin stood with her face furrowed.

"Are you sure? Maybe Cob is a nickname?"

"Well I imagine it would be, but I am certain there is no one on staff here that goes by Cob, nickname or otherwise. And as you can see, there has clearly been no one through here with a shovel for some time."

"Oh, OK," Mairin mumbled, her thoughts flurried.

"Good day to you, young lady," the woman said, then turned and headed for the bus stop. Mairin stood in a daze holding the fruitcake for two minutes before she turned around and walked into a gathering snow squall.

Over coffee and a chocolate doughnut in the window booth at Bossy's Dépanneur, Mairin decided to keep both of her recent bizarre encounters at Villa Maria from her mother for the time being. She prodded at the latest goings-on in her mind, trying to formulate a next step in an intrigue she still could not quite fully fathom.

When Mairin eventually opened the door to her mother's house, she was greeted by the familiar Christmas sensations that had drawn a warm heartline through her twenty-one years — the living room lit only by the playful illumination of strung lights on the tree. The smell of the tree, the earthy sweetness of gingerbread wafting down the hall. The musty bass note of wet wool, and the fireplace. The tinny, jingling mirth from the radio. Her mother's warm smile.

Elaine floated into the room and placed an orange paper crown on Mairin's head, then handed her a mug that she knew contained Christmas cheer. Mairin put down the fruitcake, took off her sodden outer garments and let them fall in a heap. Her mother tisked.

"Maaaa, I can't wear a crown unless I crack a cracker! Gimme a cracker," Mairin said, then blew her runny nose. Elaine gave her daughter a gold foil Christmas cracker, and the two settled in on the couch. Mairin pulled open the cracker with a pop.

"Oh Mair, this guy from McGill called for you. A Rodney — said something about the bird club thing. He asked if you had figured out your white mystery bird. He sounded sweet on you, you know."

"Ah no, Ma, he wasn't sweet on me. Thanks," Mairin said, focused on sorting through the contents she had liberated from inside her cracker.

"So did you? Figure it out?"

"Yeah Ma, it was nothing, just an albino sparrow. Mystery solved."

"OK," Elaine said, not looking entirely convinced.

"Did he leave a number? The Rodney guy?" Mairin said. Her mother raised her eyebrows and laughed.

With a goofy grin, Mairin held up a red whistle and a small metal goose, then raised her mug to the fireplace.

"Here's to you, Murray. And you too, Cob."

"Why did you say Cob? That was your grandfather's nickname in the war. Was that in his notes?" Elaine said.

"Um, yeah," Mairin said quietly.

Elaine passed a small framed picture to Mairin.

"I finally found his picture yesterday morning when I was

cleaning out a box from the move. Here he is, your grandfather Murray in his uniform. The Grenadier Guards. Isn't he handsome?"

Mairin looked into the face of the man in the officer's cap, and her spine coated with adrenal ice. The nose, the hairline, the kindness of the face. She was looking at a picture of Cob, the groundskeeper, as a much younger man. She swallowed hard.

"He's a kind man," Mairin said. Elaine cocked her head.

"He was a kind man, I heard, wasn't he?" Mairin said.

Frank Sinatra crooned *The First Noel* on the radio. Mairin put down the picture.

"Mhhh-hmm," Elaine said.

"Tell me more about him," Mairin said, regaining her outward composure.

Elaine checked the clock on the mantel and slid her daughter a present wrapped in baby blue paper specked with silver snowflakes.

"Ooh, I know it's not midnight yet, but close enough. Open it up, honey."

"Merry Christmas, Ma."

"Mairin Christmas, hun."

Mairin rolled her eyes and unwrapped her present. It was a cigar box stuffed with letters, and several small notebooks.

"I didn't know him very well myself, Mair, he passed on when I was quite young, as you know. Maybe these will help. I found them when I dug out that picture. Kind of a surprise present for you."

"Wowee," Mairin said, and inspected a notebook that had **Strange birds I saw in France 1916–1917** and another with **Birds NDG 1906–1911** printed on the cover in Murray Nolan's distinctive green handwriting.

"It's some of his wartime letters, and it looks like more of the notes he took about his birdwatching. Would you like to have these?"

"Yes Ma, I would love to have these."

Mairin's fingers detected deep grooves on the back of one of the books, and flipped it over, revealing the words "Studia vestra sunt momenti. Numquam dedite," carved deeply with repeated pen strokes.

"Studia vestra sunt momenti, Numquam dedite," Elaine laughed. "... one of dad's many poorly-translated Latin mottos that he lived by: Your studies are important, never quit."

I guess I won't, Mairin thought, then she flipped over a third notebook that had a yellowed label that read **Complete North- -ern Cardinal migration data** pasted onto the front cover, slightly askew.

Mairin felt like she could not take in a breath for a long moment. She wanted to tell her mother that this single notebook could very well prove that Murray Nolan had formulated several groundbreaking ornithological theories and that Dr. Drouin had stolen these ideas — but she did not. Instead, she hugged her mother, and thought of how her semester had not been a total write-off, and about how she was going to beg her professors at Bishop's to let her do makeup work so she could pass those classes she was in the process of failing. She also wondered how much a decent camera with a telephoto lens would set her back.

"Studia vestra sunt momenti, Numquam dedite, Ma," Mairin said with a smile, her eyes tearing up. She picked up the cigar box and hugged it to her chest for dramatic effect, then the two clinked mugs and sang along to the end of the song.

-End-

MATT POLL - AUTHOR

One crisp spring evening, on a remote island in the Yellow Sea, a Korean gangster kidnapped me and forced me to drink tree alcohol with him. We ended up singing John Denver songs together until sunrise. True story. That's what it took for me to recognize my calling. As I shambled home that morning, it hit me —
"I need to start writing some of this down."

A migratory Montréaler who has returned home after over a decade abroad, Matt Poll's background lies in academia. However, his travels led him to new pursuits — birds, writing, proofreading, and even Karaoke. Recognizing that everyone has a story, Matt knew after that night of revelry that he had more than his fair share.

DAN SVATEK - ARTIST

Dan Svatek has been doodling all manner of creatures since he was first able to hold a pencil. Drawing stories about the escapades of a beloved pet parakeet led to a lifelong fascination with birds and birdwatching. After many years as an illustrator and storyboard artist, Dan has more recently turned his attention to comics and animal portraiture, inspired by the rescued farm animals at the SAFE sanctuary in Quebec. Dan recently presented an exhibition of paintings in Montreal entitled "Cutting Board Portraits" based on these rescued animals. His upcoming graphic novel, "Cat Looker", is supported by a grant from the Canada Council.

MORE FROM MATT POLL

Dark Flock isn't your average novel. It's a curated collection of freaky feathered fiction. From post-apocalyptic birding expeditions to eerie encounters with surreal avian forces, each story in this collection will leave you questioning reality. Join characters as they navigate through twisted narratives set in Denmark, Korea, and beyond, where the line between the natural and the supernatural blurs. With a blend of mystery, dystopia, and paranormal, "Dark Flock" promises to captivate readers with its unique concepts in Matt Poll's world of Twilight Zone Birding.

Manufactured by Amazon.ca
Acheson, AB

14940096R00032